THIS BOOK WAS ILLUSTRATED BY THE WALT DISNEY STUDIO
ESPECIALLY FOR GOLDEN BOOKS

The adaptation to the animated screen of the
beloved children's classic, Lewis Carroll's *Alice
in Wonderland*, has been one of the most ambi-
tious projects of the Walt Disney Studio. The
masterful blending of the familiar charm of the
original Tenniel illustrations with typical Disney
whimsy is the culmination of many years of de-
voted effort. Alice, we feel confident, will win
many new admirers in this handsome and lively
setting.

abcdefghij

Walt Disney's
Alice in Wonderland
MEETS THE WHITE RABBIT

RETOLD BY JANE WERNER
PICTURES BY THE WALT DISNEY STUDIO

ADAPTED BY AL DEMPSTER FROM THE MOTION PICTURE
BASED ON THE STORY BY LEWIS CARROLL

A GOLDEN BOOK • NEW YORK

Western Publishing Company, Inc., Racine, Wisconsin 53404

DO YOU KNOW where Wonderland is? It is the place you visit in your dreams, the strange and wondrous place where nothing is as it seems. It was in Wonderland that Alice met the White Rabbit.

He was hurrying across the meadow, looking at his pocket watch and saying to himself: "I'm late, I'm late, for an important date."

So Alice followed him.

"What a peculiar place to give a party," she thought as she pushed her way into the hollow tree.

But before she could think any more, she began
to slide on some slippery white pebbles inside.
And then
she
began
to
fall!

"Curious and curiouser!" said Alice as she floated slowly down, past cupboards and lamps, a rocking chair, past clocks and mirrors she met in mid-air.

By the time she reached the bottom, and landed
with a thump, the White Rabbit was disappearing
through a tiny little door, too small for Alice to
follow him.

Poor Alice! She was all alone in Wonderland, where nothing was just what it seemed. (You know how things are in dreams!)

She met other animals, yes, indeed, strange talking animals, too. They tried to be as helpful as they could. But they couldn't help her find the White Rabbit.

"And I really must find him," Alice thought, though she wasn't sure just why.

So on she wandered through Wonderland, all by her lonely self.

At last she reached a neat little house in the woods, with pink shutters and a little front door that opened and—out came the White Rabbit!

"Oh, my twitching whiskers!" he was saying to
himself. He seemed very much upset. Then he looked
up and saw Alice standing there.

"Mary Ann!" he said sharply. "Why, Mary Ann, what are you doing here? Well, don't just do something, stand there! No, go get my gloves. I'm very late!"

"But late for what? That's just what I—" Alice began to ask.

"My gloves!" said the White Rabbit firmly. And Alice dutifully went to look for them, though she knew she wasn't Mary Ann!

When she came back, the White Rabbit was just
disappearing through the woods again.

So off went Alice, trying to follow him through that strange, mixed-up Wonderland.

She met Tweedledee and Tweedledum, a funny little pair.

She joined a mad tea party with the Mad Hatter
and the March Hare.

She met a Cheshire cat who faded in and out of sight. And one strange creature–Jabberwock–whose eyes flamed in the night.

They all were very kind, but they could not show Alice the way, until:

"There *is* a short cut," she heard the Cheshire cat say. So Alice took it.

The short cut led into a garden where gardeners were busy painting roses red.

"We must hurry," they said, "for the Queen is coming!"

And sure enough, a trumpet blew, and a voice called:

"Make way for the Queen of Hearts!"

Then out came a grand procession. And who should be the royal trumpeter for the cross-looking Queen but the White Rabbit, all dressed up and looking very fine.

"Well!" said Alice. "So this is why he was hurrying so!"

"Who are you?" snapped the Queen. "Do you play croquet?"

"I'm Alice. And I'm just on my way home. Thank you for the invitation, but I really mustn't stay."

"So!" cried the Queen. "So she won't play! Off
with her head then!"

But Alice was tired of Wonderland now, and all
its nonsensical ways.

"Pooh!" she said. "I'm not frightened of you.
You're nothing but a pack of cards."

And with that she ran back through that land of dreams, back to the river bank where she had fallen asleep.

"Hm," she said, as she rubbed her eyes. "I'm glad to be back where things are what they seem. I've had quite enough for now of Wonderland!"